I0757488

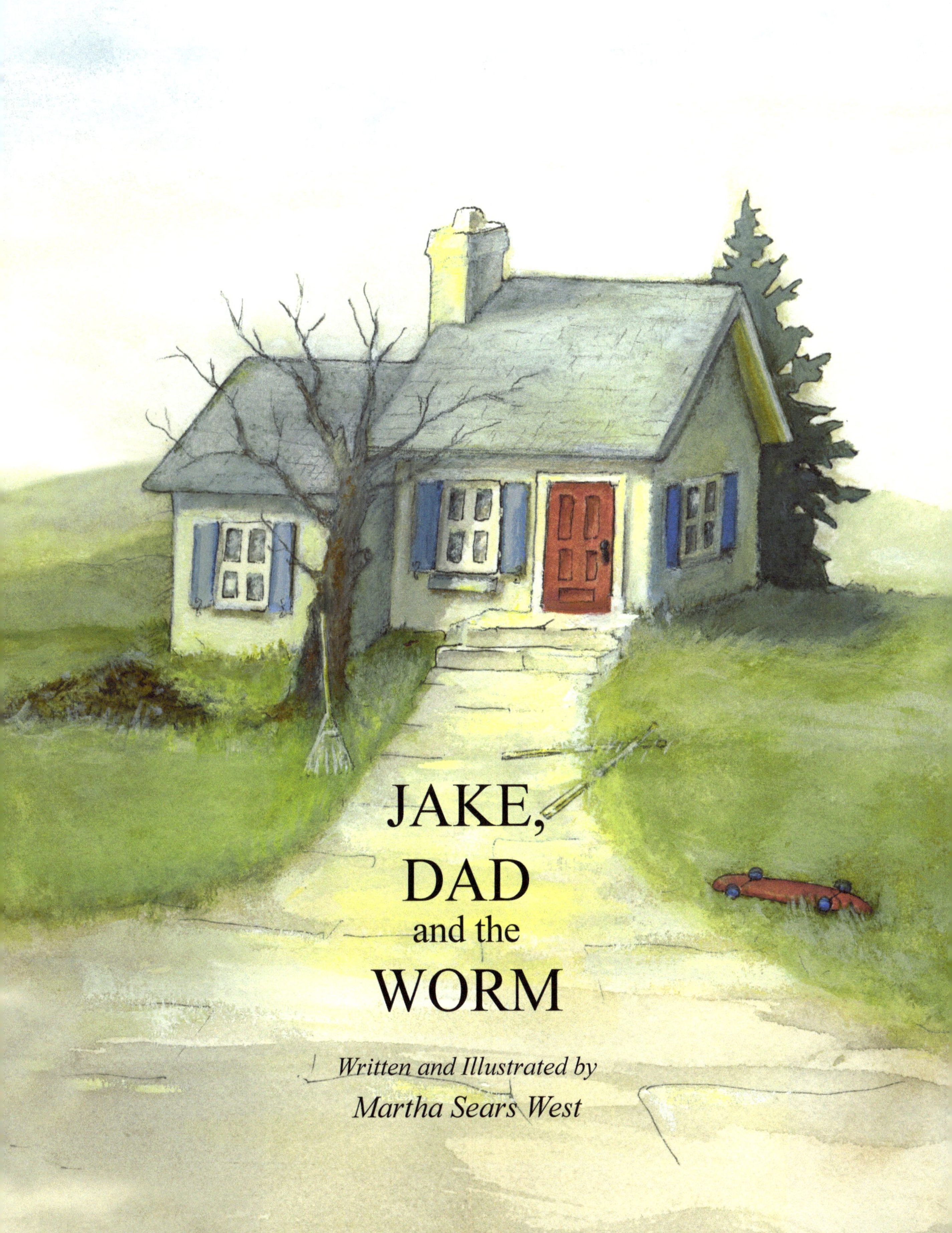

JAKE,
DAD
and the
WORM

Written and Illustrated by
Martha Sears West

CLEAN KIND WORLD
Los Angeles

Copyright © 2020 by Martha Sears West · Distributed by Ingram Book Company
Jake, Dad and the Worm. All rights reserved.
Library of Congress Control Number 2012954873
ISBN: 978--9886784-5-3 (casebound); 978-1-4751899-1-5 (softbound)
CleanKindWorldBooks.com   ParkPlacePress.com   ymaddox@CleanKindWorldBooks.com
Toll Free 800-616-8081 · Shipping 435-764-4545 · Fax 323-953-9850
2016 Cummings · Los Angeles, CA 90027

All titles are available online and in fine bookstores.
The Hetty series is available in print audio, and eBook.
Jacques and the Forgotten Christmas · *Longer Than Forevermore*
Jake, Dad and the Worm · *Rhymes and Doodles from a Wind-up Toy*
Hetty · *Hetty Happens* · *Hetty or Not* · *Honeymoon Summer* · *Hetty on Hold* · *It's Me, Pippa!*

10 9 8 7 6 5 4
Printed in the United States of America

One fall when Jake was small,
you see, the story goes like this:
His skateboard hit a little tree
he'd rather hoped to miss.

And then there were the stilts
  he thought would maximize his height,

Until he got his left leg
  kind of mixed up with his right.

So there was nothing left, he thought,
   but playing his kazoo.
Performing for the family
   was the only thing to do.

The baby didn't seem to feel
the need to hear him play;

When he was through verse number two,
his sister slipped away.

He felt a little smaller
    than he even had before,
So Jake went out to look for Dad,
    and slowly closed the door.

His dad was raking in the yard,
    with lots of work to do,
But when he looked at Jake,
    he said, "I'd rather be with you."

They nestled in a pile of leaves
and tossed them in their hair.

They smelled the dark and woody earth
and sweetness of the air.

"I wish I could be big," said Jake,
"and good at doing stuff.
When there are things I want to do,
I'm never big enough."

His dad leaned back against a tree,
his hands behind his head
Nice and easy as could be,
and this is what he said:

"When there is something hard to do,
    don't worry if you fail.
If you're afraid you'll hit your thumb,
    you'll never drive a nail.

"Although you can't do everything,
        and wish you were a man,
You're learning very well
        to do your best at what you can…"

Just then they saw the worm
        that had been crawling on a step.
He'd left a dampened streak behind
        where he'd already crept.

And Dad explained that if it's rained
        while he was underground,
A worm must wiggle up for air
        to keep from being drowned.

"What he does best is to digest
what once upon a time
Were living plants and things
that are no longer in their prime.

"When this organic matter
	has been passed throughout his coil,
We find he's turned the dirt into…
	Shazam!!! A better soil.

"Yet he can't play a red kazoo,
    or even try to hum;
Can't wear a pair of racing shoes,
    or ever hope to run.

"He cannot order hamburgers
    with pickles on the side.
When someone wants to dance with him,
    he isn't qualified.

"And when he's in the open air
      where we have lots of fun,
He's more exposed to danger
      and could shrivel in the sun."

Then suddenly elastic,
  and gymnastic, what is more,
The worm was doing many things
  they'd never seen before.

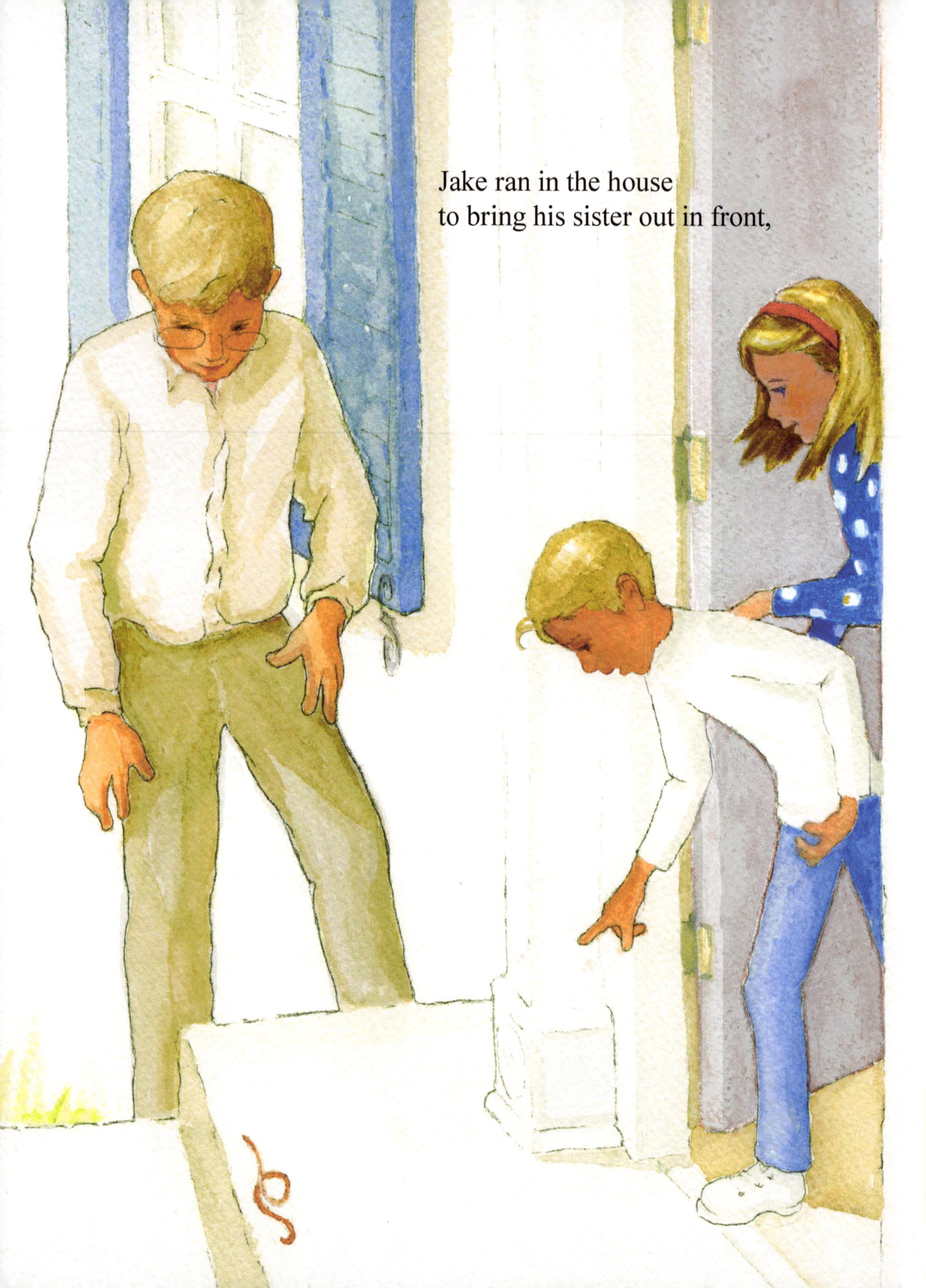

Jake ran in the house
to bring his sister out in front,

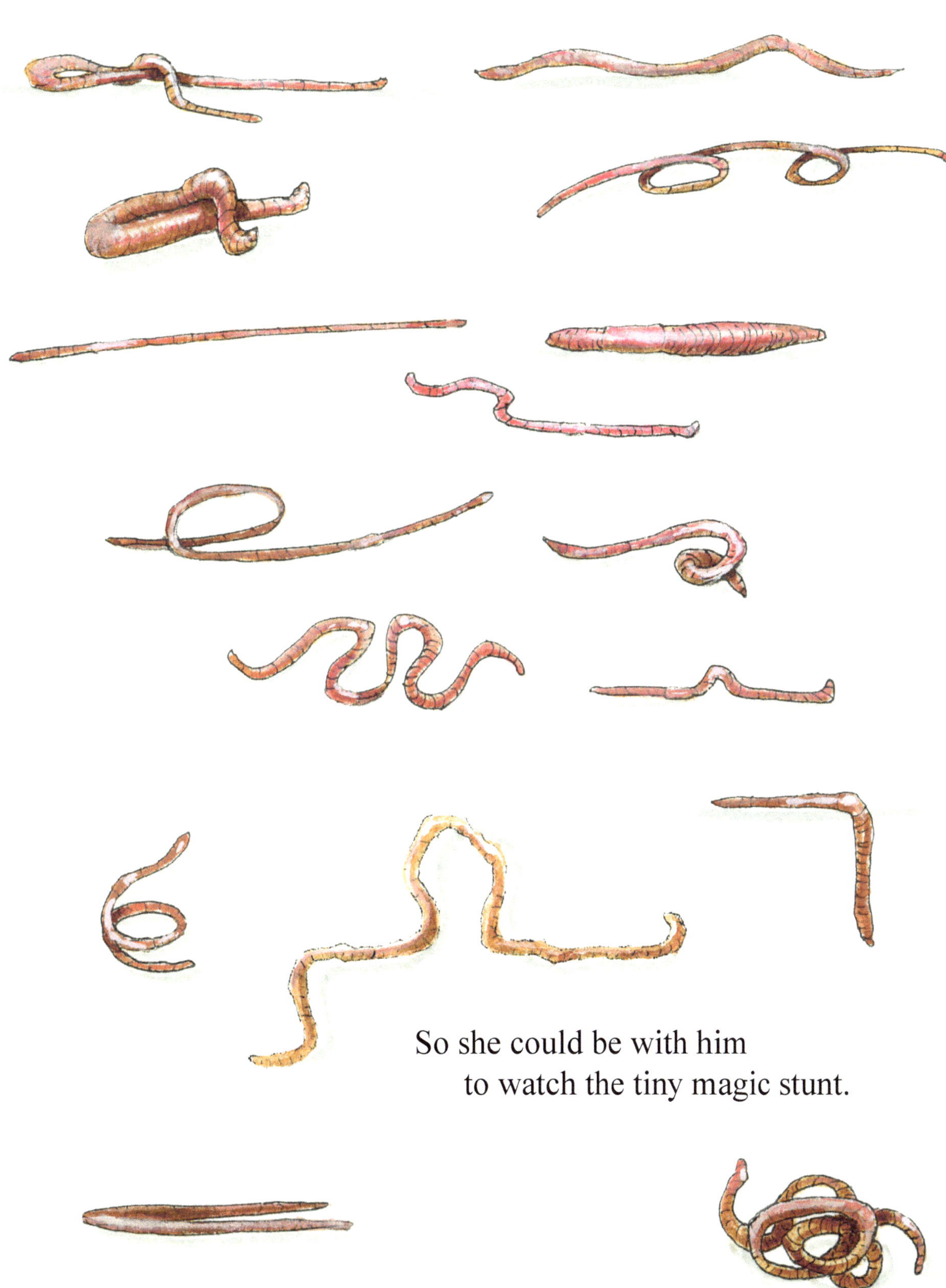

So she could be with him
to watch the tiny magic stunt.

"It's better than the zoo!
It's like a circus!"
they exclaimed.

His sister said,
"I really wish
an earthworm
could be tamed!"

They watched him slip inside himself,
   just like a double sleeve;
Not till the front moved onward,
   did the rear decide to leave.

But when he started to descend,
   not knowing what was there,
Below him he could only sense
   an awful lot of air.

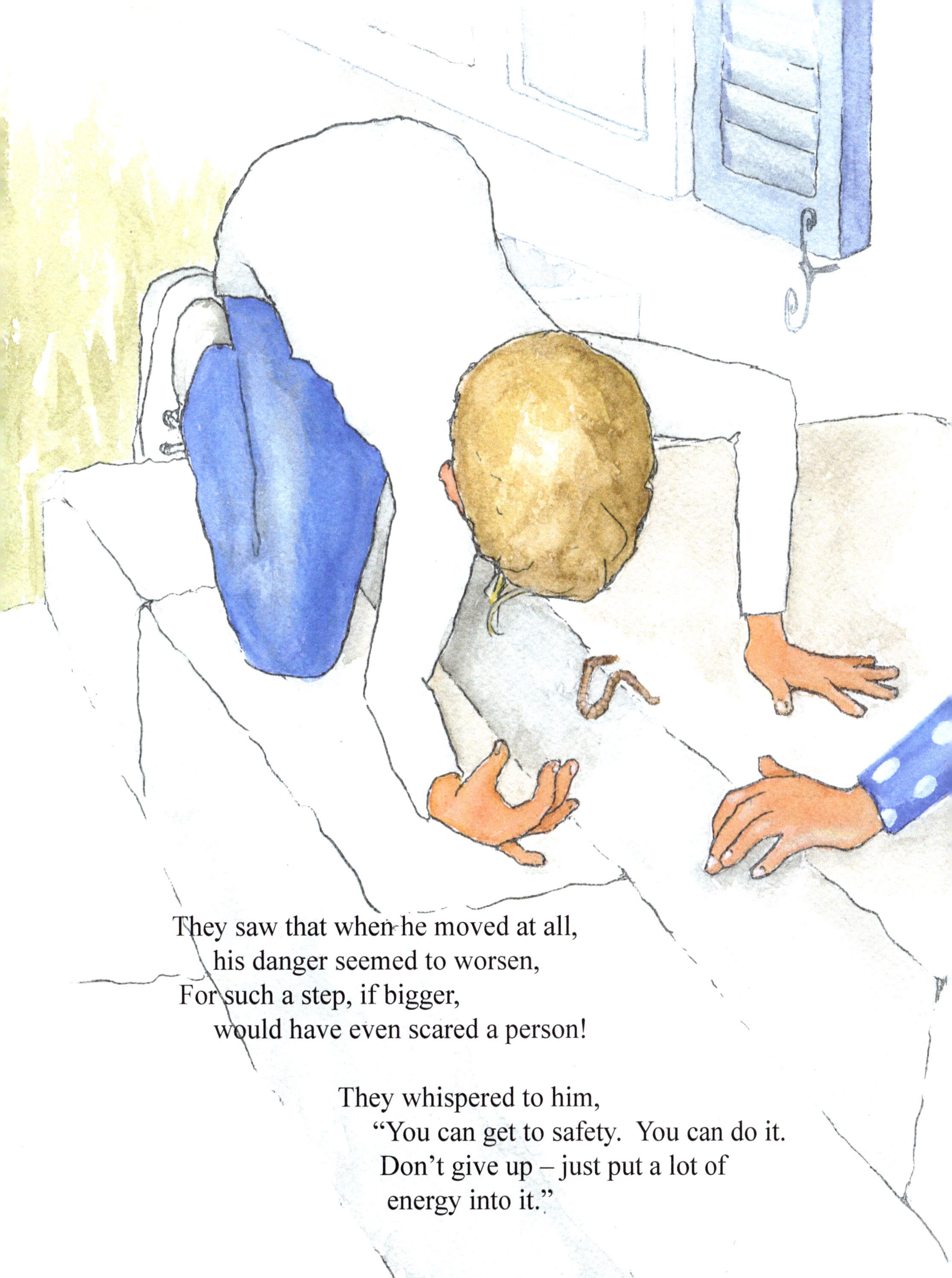

They saw that when he moved at all,
    his danger seemed to worsen,
For such a step, if bigger,
    would have even scared a person!

They whispered to him,
    "You can get to safety. You can do it.
    Don't give up – just put a lot of
        energy into it."

The front of him appeared confused–
unless it was the rear.
Which one was the caboose end,
and which the engineer?

He swung and flapped as soon as he
could muster all his powers.
They sung and clapped and brought him
grass and tiny purple flowers.

They hollered, "Be courageous!"
when they saw his middle droop,
Supposing if they cheered him on,
he'd find a way, but OOPS!

Suddenly, as if in fear,
he seemed to realize
That soon he might be trying
wings and halo on for size.

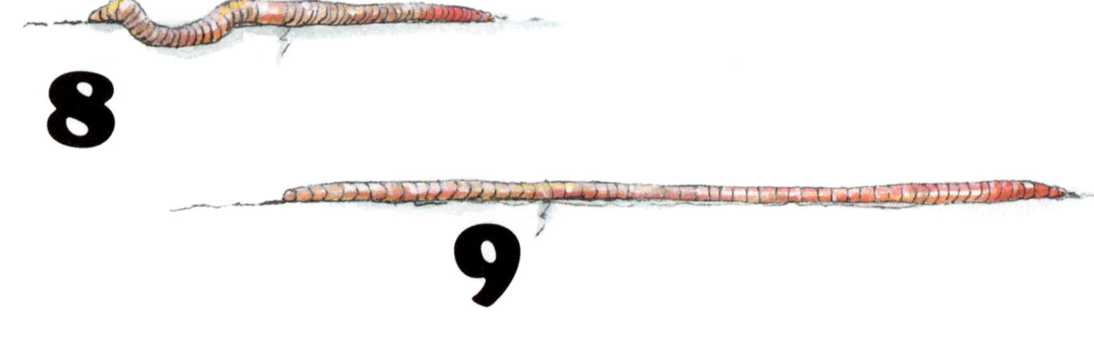

And struggling forth with energy,
not ever giving in,
He labored hard at where to go
instead of where he'd been

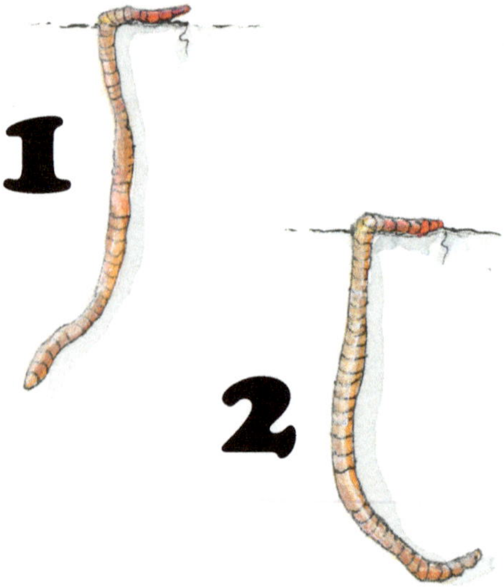

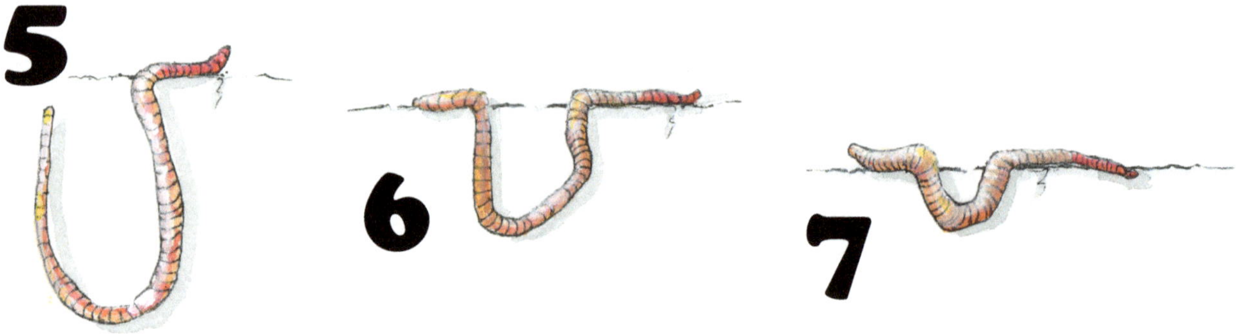

Then squared his front to bear the brunt
against the dreaded ledge,
Rolled up his sleeve to give a heave
and charged above the edge!

Although the worm had no such thing,
   he *seemed* to cock his ear,
Then wriggling forth into the grass,
   he waved his tiny rear.

He didn't win a trophy,
   though he'd worked with all his might
And got just where he ought to be,
   to everyone's delight.

* *"I shall find a way or I will make one"* is the motto of a school
known to have its land improved by worms just like this one!

Then Dad asked, " You remember
when you said you felt so small?

To see you with the worm,
  you looked
Immensely huge and tall.

"You can play a red kazoo,
    and whistle, hum, and sing.
You can run in racing shoes
    as fast as anything!

"You can order hamburgers
    with pickles on the side.
When someone needs
    some jumping done,
    you're more than qualified."

Often there are piles of leaves
that get so hard to rake
That Dad must ask if he could have
some special help from Jake.

When Jake's been working very hard,
Dad gives the biggest smile!
He knows, though Jake is tired,
he is thinking all the while…

About the worm that didn't ever
    quit till he was through,
And though he's small,
    there's still an awful lot that he can do.

THE END

Dedication

The earthworm's an invertebrate
Whose bones add up to zero;
In spite of being spineless,
He's something of a hero.
How fortunate it is for us
His Maker didn't bungle
By putting leeches in our lawns,
And worms just in the jungle.
-M.S.W.

Naturalist Charles Darwin wrote this of the worm:

"...it may be doubted if there are any other animals which have played such an important part in the history of the world as these lowly organized creatures."